The King
of the
Golden City

The King
of the Golden City

An Allegory for Children

Mother Mary Loyola
of the Bar Convent, York

Illustrated by John Watson Davis

Little Way Press

Twain Harte, California

The King of the Golden City was originally published by
P.J. Kennedy & Sons in 1921.

© 2004, 2006 Little Way Press
Cover and interior design by *osprey*design

ISBN: 0-9764691-0-3
ISBN-13: 978-0-9764691-0-X

Little Way Press
Twain Harte, California
www.littlewaypress.com

Distributed by Catholic Heritage Curricula
P.O. Box 125, Twain Harte, CA 95383
1-800-490-7713 www.chcweb.com

A study guide for *The King of the Golden City* may be downloaded
from "Free Catholic Curricula" at: www.chcweb.com

Nihil Obstat:
    Arthurus J. Scanlan, S.T.D.
        Censor Liborum
Imprimatur:
    Patritius J. Hayes, D.D.
        Archiepiscopus Neo-Eboracensis
Neo-Eboraci
die 25, Augusti 1921

Contents

1

The Meeting
in the Wood

THERE was once a King who lived in a Land where the most lovely flowers bloomed always. His Palace of ivory stood in the midst of a City through which flowed a river clear as crystal. The streets of the City were of pure gold, and the gates were a single pearl each. There was no death nor pain, nor mourning nor crying within those gates, but songs of joy resounded on every side.

Very different from this Land was another which also belonged to the King. It was a country of travelers. Its people were journeying to the Golden City and there were many troubles on the way. The King loved the poor exiles. He tried to keep them safe from harm and to make them happy as far as he could. But to make them quite happy, without any dangers or pain—this he could not do; first, because the country through which they were passing was not meant to be their home, and next because of a certain rebel lord, named Malignus, who lived there. He had once been a servant of the King but had turned against him, and for the hate he bore him, he tried to harm the poor people whom the King loved. The home of the exiles was the Beautiful Land where the King himself lived with all the Happy Ones who had spent their time of exile well and had loved and served their King.

Now it chanced that as the King was wandering one day in a dark wood of the Land of Exile, he came upon a little maid of eight or nine. She was very poor and her clothes, though tidy, were threadbare. She lived in a hut hard by. Whether it was the King's fancy and nothing more, certain it is that he was drawn to the little maid. He had no sooner seen her than he loved her and longed to make her happy, and this at any cost to himself. He spoke kindly to her, took the heavy bundle of faggots off her shoulders, made her sit down by his side on the trunk of a fallen tree, and tell him all about herself and her troubles. When it was time for her to go, he arranged her load so that it was easy for her to carry, and when she turned her head for a last look at him, he was still following her with his kind eyes as if he was sorry to part with her.

After this he would often come to her in the wood, and each time she came to know him better and to love him more. He told her that if she liked, he would take her to his own Beautiful Land where she would be with him always and have everything her heart desired. It could not be at once because she must be trained to be a fit companion for the princes and princesses of the Golden City. But to comfort her till the happy time came, he would often come to see her and he would teach her himself what she would have to learn. In the City everyone was like him: she would have to become like him before she could live amongst them. He would teach her in his visits and would bring her rich presents that she might not be ashamed to be presented at his Court.

One day he gave her a great surprise. He said he was coming to meet her, not in the wood, but in her own little hut, that he

might see for himself all she wanted and give her whatever was good for her to have. He spoke so kindly and looked at her so lovingly, that she was sure he meant all he said. Yet she could not help saying:

"How is it, O great King, that with so many grand folks and faithful friends about you, you should care to come to a poor little maid like me?" And he said:

"I loved you long before you ever heard of me, and if you will love me in return I shall think myself repaid for all I have done for you and am going to do. You have nothing costly to give me, but there are wild flowers you can offer me. Bring them into your hut and they will please me."

She was delighted and prepared the little place carefully for his coming. The floor was only mud but she swept it clean. She made the one tiny window clear and bright, and drew within a trailing rose that its fragrance might refresh the King. And then she went and hunted diligently for the wild flowers that he loved, the humble violet, the roses with their thorny stems, and, above all, the sweet forget-me-nots. She came home with her apron full. She was tired, for it had cost her something to get her treasures. But she did not mind the trouble if only she could please the King and make him some return for the long journey he would have to take to come to her. She had heard that the treasures he was bringing her had not cost him nothing, nay, that he had had to work hard and go through dreadful pain to purchase them. Could she ever do enough for him?

He came. Not in all his majesty as he was known in the Golden City—that would only have frightened her—but in a simple robe of white, so disguised that some foolish people who knew how great was the King of the Golden City, mocked and said that this meek and lowly stranger could not be he.

He came. And you should have seen his smile when he saw the little hut. There was a path through the wood to it all strewn with flowers. At the door the little maid was waiting for him with outstretched arms. And she brought him into the hut. And the door was shut.

I cannot tell you what passed between them during the quarter of an hour he was within. That is their secret. But when the King came out, the maid's beaming face told what a happy time they had had together. The white robe she had taken care to put on, was all sparkling with jewels—his gifts to her, no doubt. Anyone quite near the door would have heard her say: "Lord, come again soon." She watched him go down the flowery path until it turned and he was out of sight. Then she went in and shut the door, and had anyone been by, he would have heard her singing for days after as she went about her work:

"Come, dearest King, again to me,
How much, how much I long for thee."

And he came again, and again. Each time the flowery path was ready, each time the rose trailed through the open pane; each time the forget-me-nots lay about his feet as he and the little maid sat together, hand in hand.

The fifth time—or was it the sixth?—he noticed that the gay path to the hut was shorter, and the flowers less fresh than usual. Perhaps the little maid was tiring of a preparation that must cost something. Anyhow, the King's quick eye noted the change, and a sigh escaped him. Next time he missed the flowers within the hut. He did not complain but his smile was a little sad. After that, his welcome grew less hearty each time he came. He did not get the invitations that were once so pressing, and on the days of his visit the little maid did not fill the place with her song. There was scarcely any preparation for him now. When he came the hut was—not dirty, of course—but dusty and uncared for. And he looked in vain for the flowers. He did not change. He brought his rich gifts as usual. But there was no fit spot to lay them down. So he took them away with him, and kept them for the little maid in hopes of better times. And the old times did return.

The King came one day as usual—down no flowery pathway now. She was not standing in the doorway but amusing herself within. He had to stoop as he went in, for above and around cobwebs were clinging everywhere. She greeted him, to be sure, and said she was glad to see him, but in a minute or two she got up from her place at his feet and wandered about outside.

Suddenly, a village clock chimed the quarter. It was the time his visits came to a close. And she was not with him! She had left him alone, the friend who had come so far for her sake. The thought of her carelessness and ingratitude rushed upon her. Oh, how could she have been so thoughtless, so unkind! She hurried back to the hut to tell him of her sorrow. But the door was open—he had gone. Gone after such a visit! Oh, what could she do to make it up to him? How different were these last visits from the first in which she had made him so welcome! Could she ever ask him to come again?

Yes, she knew him and she did not despair. Not only would she invite him again, but the welcome should be so hearty as to remind him of their first meeting. She set to work bravely. The hut was scoured and the walls were cleaned. She was tired, but she did not mind—it was for the King. And then, the flowers. She was surprised to find how easily they came to hand. They had not to be fetched from afar, for they lay thick around the hut in every direction and only waited gathering. As to the roses, what if the thorns did prick and make her fingers bleed? They were for the King. She would not mind the pain. And he would know, when he saw them, that she had borne the smart for his sake.

Really, when all was ready, the hut looked quite a picture—very poor, of course, but so cared for, so bright. The flowery path was long and gay as on the first glad day. And she longed so to tell him of her sorrow and her love, that it seemed as if

the time for his visit would never come. As he crossed the little threshold under the roses, she sank at his feet and her tears fell among the flowers. How tenderly he raised her, and listened as she told him of her sorrow, and comforted and forgave her! When she asked him what she could do to make up for her carelessness in the past, he said:

"Give me your heart. Love makes up for everything. Love me. Make ready for me in the little ways you know I like. Never mind the trouble and the pain. I have borne pain and trouble for you." And he showed her great wounds which he told her had been caused by his love for her. She listened, she promised, and because she knew herself to be a little coward, she asked him to help her. And so the old times came back. He was made welcome as before. Not that she was always as careful as she might have been. Oh, no! She was often thoughtless and lazy. But when she had failed, she was sorry and told the King at once. She knew him so well now, and trusted him so fully and was so sure of his love for her that she was not afraid to tell him everything she had done—even the things that were most displeasing to him—since he was with her last. He was always patient with her. He was never tired of forgiving her as soon as she was sorry. He taught her what he wanted her to know so that, gradually, she might grow like him and be made ready for her place in the Golden City.

2

The Little Maid Finds She Must Help in Her Own Training

I ought to have told you that the name of the little maid was Flos. This means "a flower," and indeed she was a little wild flower for many a long day. There was much to be improved in her. She forgot her promises, she was willful and selfish, so provoking at times that you and I would have given her up and told the King that she would never make a princess. Those into whose charge he had given her, did say so. But the King only smiled. He loved her too much to give her up. He did not spoil her. But he made much of every little improvement, praised her when she tried to please him, and when she had displeased him, forgave her as soon as she was sorry.

At their first meeting he had told her that if she wished he would take her some day to be with him in the Golden City. She was enchanted and went about saying to herself that she was to be a princess and have grand robes and jewels and do just as she liked. She told the King how glad she was and that she wished the time would come quickly.

He listened quietly and said:

"Dilecta, (this was his name for her) I have told you that *if you wish* you shall be with me in my Palace, but you must be ready to pay the price."

"The price?" she replied sadly, "but I am so poor."

"I have paid the price of your place there," he answered, "but I cannot do all. Those who really wish to be with me there must get ready."

"How, dear King?"

"By keeping my laws and learning how to know and love and serve me. This is what the Happy Ones did during their time of exile. They worked hard, and when I came to take them to their true country, they were ready. You must be trained, Dilecta, if you are to be a princess in my Court."

"I shall not mind that," she said gaily, "it must be nice to be trained by a King."

"I shall help, but a King does not do all the training of his soldiers and courtiers by himself. He has his lieutenants, or those who take his place, his instructors who teach their pupils what they have to learn. I shall give you a prince of my Court to be your Guardian, to be with you always. He will tell you what I want you to do. He will check you when you are going to do wrong, and encourage you when you are in difficulty or in danger. You must call him to your help when you are in need and you must obey and respect and love him for all his care of you. To make it easy for you to know what I want, you shall have my ten chief laws or commands, written plainly in a book, and I will give you teachers who will speak to you in my name, so that in obeying them you will obey me as if you really heard my voice."

The little maid hung down her head and looked sad.

"I would rather hear your voice, dear King," she said. "I like to do what you tell me, but I may not like to do what other people want."

"If you really love me you will want to do as I like. I know what is best for you and what you must do to make you fit to be with me in the Golden City. You will have to go to school and the lessons will be hard sometimes. The Happy Ones in my Palace had to do many things they did not like, things that hurt very much. But I helped them always, and because they loved me and trusted me, they did not mind the pain. They tried their best to keep my laws and to do all that I told them, either myself, or by their Prince Guardian, or the teachers I sent. You, too, must love and trust me, Dilecta."

She did not answer but laid her hand in his.

3

The King's Laws

I am afraid you will think Dilecta a selfish, silly little thing, and wonder what the King saw in her to love. There was certainly a great deal in her that he could not love. He saw that she was willful and changeable, and that she loved him more for the presents he gave her, and for those he promised her, than for himself. But he saw, too, something which no one else could see, something beautiful and lovable that she would become if she would fight against the ugly things he could not love. He loved what she would be one day when her training was finished, and so he had patience with her and put up with her trying ways.

The very next time she saw him after their last talk she began:

"Dear King, I do so wish you would take me now, this minute, to the Golden City, and that I might not have to keep laws and do things that hurt. Why must there be laws for people who want to be good?"

It was one of her foolish questions, but the King took the trouble to explain because this was a matter that concerned the little maid very much, and if you care about her you must try to understand it as she had to do.

If you ask which is the happiest country in the world today, you will be told it is where there are laws to keep the good people safe and happy, and to punish the bad. And if you want to know where the people are most miserable, you will find it is

where there is anarchy, or no government, where cruel, selfish men do as they like, and rob and kill without anyone being strong enough to prevent or punish them. Laws are not made to tease and trouble people but to keep them from harm.

There were laws even in the King's own country, and it was because the Happy Ones there kept them perfectly that they were quite happy and had everything they could wish, without any trouble or pain. But this perfect peace and joy could not be found even by good people in the Land of Exile. Malignus, who had been the first to break the King's laws and whom the King was obliged to punish for his disobedience, did all he could to get those who were traveling toward the Golden City to break the laws too, that they might be punished with him. He hated to think that they were on their way to the beautiful home he had lost. So he tried to get them to be disobedient like himself. He could not *make* them do wrong, but he could advise and coax them. And this is how he did it.

In country places where two or more roads meet, a signpost is put up to guide the passersby. Wise travelers consult it and carefully follow its directions. They do not look out for the pleasantest but for the safest and shortest route to their journey's end. In the Land of Exile, signposts bearing the King's commands were set up at the parting of ways, that all men might know which road would bring them to their true Country.

To dissuade them from taking it, Malignus stood at the crossroads to point out the attractions of the broad road and the hardships of the narrow way. By watching the travelers all through their journey, he had come to know them well. He saw that because they all liked what was most easy and comfortable, they were often in danger of leaving the straight road to the Golden City. So he tried to persuade them that it was hard to have to climb a steep hill when there was a flowery path close by. He could not *make* them choose the easier way—do remember this—but he could try to prove that to be happy we must do what costs us least. This is a great mistake. The Happy Ones who reached the Home the King had ready for them, got there by trying to do always what the King wanted of them for their good. They would not listen to Malignus, nor to their own likes and dislikes. They gave ear to their dear King and Leader saying to them:

"If you love me keep my commandments. And keep them, too, for your own sake. I ask you for a little while to go against yourselves sometimes, for your own good. When I get you safely to our true Home, I will never ask you to do anything hard any more."

Perhaps you will say or think: "Yes, when they got to the Golden City they were happy of course, but they had to be unhappy all the way there."

Far from it. The good people were happy even as they traveled along the hard road. They were even happier than the people on the easy road who were always trying to please themselves and shun labor and pain. The Land of Exile was a place of trial *for all,* but the good people did not have to bear more than the bad. Shall I tell you why? All along the hard and narrow road the good King had placed things to help the travelers but Malignus didn't care whether the people on his broad road suffered or not.

Before the King met the little maid, she was like a wild colt running about as it likes, doing no work, and of no use to anyone. But after he had taken her in hand, she had often to say "No" to herself. You must remember that the King had offered her a great reward if she would let herself be prepared to be a princess in his Court. It was a matter that rested with herself. He would not force her against her will. If she refused to be trained, he would make the offer to someone else with more sense and thankfulness for his kindness. All through her time of training she could do as she chose—keep the King's laws or not: she had free will.

He explained this clearly to Dilecta. But he had often to repeat the same thing, she was so apt to be led by likes or dislikes. It was only by degrees that she began to ask herself: "What would my dear King like? If I do this, shall I be glad or sorry next time I see him?" And then she would do the right thing bravely and not mind the pain for the joy it would be to see his smile.

4

The King's Household

WE have seen that the King of the Golden City was so good and kind, that although he could do whatever he wished and had whatever he could desire—riches, joy, the love of all around him—he was not satisfied to have these good things for himself alone. He wished his subjects to be happy, too. They must be happy in the Land of Exile, so far as he could help them. They must be happy afterwards with him and all who had reached the Beautiful Land, with a perfect happiness beyond anything they could desire or even imagine.

So he was not content that the exiles should be his servants and subjects only. He wished to adopt them and make them his children, most dear children, whilst they were quite tiny. When this was done, a beautiful white robe called "Grace" was given them, and their names were written in a book called "The Book of Life." No one could take the robe from them, or blot their names out of that Book—no one *but themselves*. If their names were found written there when they reached the gates of the Golden City, they were sure to be let in.

The King had a large House in which was stored all that his subjects needed on their way to their true Country. From the child taking its first tottering steps thither, to the aged pilgrim nearing the end of the journey, all were provided for.

There was also the *School*, where the King's children were taught their duty to their Royal Father and to one another.

Maps showed them the right road to the Promised Land that they might not lose their way. And they read the history of the Land of Exile, that they might learn a lesson from the lives of the pilgrims, good and bad, who had gone before them.

There was the *Gymnasium,* where they were trained by many exercises how to use the wonderful powers given them; how to fit themselves for Active Service and defend themselves against the King's enemies and their own. Close by was the *Armory,* where they could see the sword and shield, the helmet and the breastplate, and the strong shoes they would need when they were old enough to be enrolled among the King's soldiers. Further on was the *Hospital* or *Infirmary* for the wounded and the sick.

And—most wonderful of all—there was the *Banquet Hall* for young and old, rich and poor alike; and the *Royal Audience Chamber* where the King was ready to receive at all hours those who came to him for favors, for advice, or for help in their troubles or their needs. Here, too, at certain times he would meet his friends gathered together to entertain him and praise him with music and song, and to cheer themselves with the thought of the happy time when they would leave the Land of Exile and be with him "in Patria," their own dear Country and Home.

5

A Troublesome Partner

THE people in the Land of Exile lived a good deal alone. They met together at certain times, but each one lived a large part of his or her life in a little hut which the owner had to keep swept and tidy.

I say they lived alone, but in reality all the men, women and children each had a comrade who was always with them, from the time they came into the Land till the time they went out, and forever after. The name of this partner was Self. The two were never separated. They walked, worked, went to sleep and woke together. But the owner of the hut was—or ought to have been—master or mistress there. Self was the sub-, or under-partner. So it was not what Self liked or disliked that mattered, but what the King wanted and what was good for the owner of the hut. This lesson Self had to learn, and, as a rule, it was learnt very slowly. A constant struggle for the upperhand went on, therefore, in most of the huts, and in one particularly, as we shall see.

Now, if any of you think it would have saved trouble to let Self be the ruler in every hut, that the poor owner might have the chance of a quiet life, I must tell you that you know very little about the matter. Not, mind you, that the hut-owners never tried this plan. Some of them did. Either they never fought Self at all, or they gave in after a short tussle. But sooner or later they all found out their mistakes. Once master, Self showed himself (or herself, as the case might be) a cruel tyrant. He made a slave of the hut-owner who should have taught him better, and treated him so badly that life was a misery to him. No: the only way to secure any kind of peace was to keep this unruly comrade in his place and put him down firmly when he gave himself airs.

But we must get back to one little hut and its inmates.

"Six o'clock—time to get up," said Dilecta, and she was just going to make a spring, when Self's sleepy voice was heard:

"It can't be time yet, and if it is, the clock's fast or wrong."

"It was right all day yesterday. Come, get up!"

"Oh! I am so awfully tired . . and . . and I've a head . . ache . . at least I had one yesterday . . and I don't want to . . to have one tomorr . . ow or I shan't enjoy . . the fa . . ir."

"If we don't get up we shan't get our work done. The King comes this morning, and there's the floor to sweep and the flowers to get."

"There's plen . . ty of time yet, and five minutes can't make any . . differ . . ence."

Now Dilecta had been warned again and again by the Prince Guardian not to argue with Self, especially the first thing in the morning. He said there was no lawyer to equal Self at that time. The only thing to do was to spring up at once and not listen to her. Dilecta had been listening all this time, and now she said sleepily:

"Oh, ve . . ry wel . . ll . . then . . just five minutes . . an' we'll take care to keee . . p awaak . . " So they turned over and in less than one minute were fast asleep again.

The sun was shining brightly into the hut when Dilecta woke with a start:

"Oh! how late it is. It will be too late, and it's all your fault, Self. I told you we should miss the King. And now he will have knocked and had no answer—and passed us by."

She spoke of the King, but I fancy she was more vexed with Self than sorry for his Majesty. And Self was angry, too, for she could not bear blame, especially from Dilecta. It made her feel so uncomfortable.

"It was quite as much your fault as mine," she said sharply, "and you ought to know better for you're always preaching."

They wrangled in this way all the time they were dressing, and at breakfast, and on the way to school. There everything went wrong, and no wonder, for they were not at peace together, and could not leave others in peace. One thing, however, was curious, but it is a fact. Though Dilecta was cross because Self had got the better of her in the morning, she showed her ill-temper by giving way to Self all the rest of the day. And Self, instead of being satisfied with this, got more and more discontented and disagreeable as the hours went on.

It was late that evening when the Prince Guardian, coming to Dilecta's hut, saw no light in the little window which was generally a bright patch in the darkness. There was crying within, and, opening the door, he found her sitting on the floor looking hot and angry.

"How is this, Dilecta, all in the dark. Where is your lamp?"

Now the name of that lamp was "Peace." It was the King's special gift to his friends and his directions about it were very important. It was to be kept burning at all costs. No wind nor storm was ever to put it out, and it was never to be left near the window, lest Malignus should put his hand in and take it away. He was always trying to get hold of it. He had been heard to say that he thought he had done a good day's work if he had succeeded in robbing a little child of its lamp. At times it burned rather low in Dilecta's hut, but it was never out. So you will understand the Prince Guardian's grave look and tone of reproof on finding the little place in darkness.

"How is this?" he asked again.

"Ma . . lignus," she sobbed, "it was Malignus. I had it too near the window, and he's got it. And . . and it was nearly out before he took it." And she burst out crying again.

"Get up now and tell me all about it."

"Oh, Prince, it's been such a bad day! When I woke it was raining and cold, and the first thing I saw were Self's sleepy eyes looking very sorry for me. 'Dilecta', she said, 'don't get up just yet. You're tired, and Monday's a horrid day, there's nothing to look forward to. Wait a bit'. So I waited and waited till I fell asleep again. When I did get up everything went wrong. We were late for school and when we were scolded I said what wasn't true. The lessons were too hard and all the teachers were unkind and the children too. I was cross with Self all day, but somehow I let her do just as she wanted as if I didn't care what I did. When I came home it was too dark to see to do anything, and I didn't care to trim my lamp, and it burned lower and lower. And then—suddenly—I saw a hand come out of the darkness and snatch it away. Oh, my lamp, my lamp! And the King gave it to me and told me to take care of it." And she began sobbing afresh.

The Prince Guardian listened patiently. Then he said:

"I have spoken to you many times today, Dilecta, but you would not listen to me. When I spoke you turned away, and see what has come of it. But you have owned up now like a good child, and you have learned a useful lesson. You have found out that when Malignus and Self advise you to do as you like and have your own way in everything, it is not to make you happy, as they pretend, but to get what they want themselves. Self wants to have some pleasure or to get rid of some pain or trouble that very minute. It is not you she is thinking about at all. Malignus wants to make you sad and discouraged, and this is the way he sets about it. He tries to make you do wrong and break the King's laws just to please yourself. 'It's only a little thing', he whispers, 'It doesn't matter much'. Watch, now, and see what he does next. If you listen to him and do as he advises, he turns upon you directly and says: 'Now you've done it. You've broken your resolutions again. You are always breaking them and you'll never be any better. So it's no use trying, and you may as well give it all up and just enjoy yourself. You're a mean, ungrateful little thing and the King is tired of you'."

Dilecta looked up surprised.

"I thought it was you, Prince, who tried to make me sorry when I broke my resolutions and made the King sad."

"No, my child. I try to make you sorry for having displeased the King. But the Prince Guardians never discourage the children they have charge of. No matter how often they fall, we always cheer them up and tell them to go on as before. You may fail hundreds of times. But what of that! Your faults are no worse because you see them better. When the ugly measle-marks show themselves, you say: 'Oh, how frightful!' But the doctor is quite pleased and says they are much better outside than inside. They will soon go away now. So to see what is ugly in yourself is a sign of better things coming. The King never discourages you, Dilecta. He is very gentle and patient with you. And he wants you to be patient with yourself. You cannot correct all your faults at once. If you work at this task as long as you are in the Land of Exile, it is what you were sent here to do. And when the task is done, you will go Home to the Golden City for the holidays."

"Oh, look, look!" cried Dilecta joyfully, "my lamp has come back. Whilst you were talking and telling me to cheer up, I saw

it put in its place again, and it's getting brighter and brighter. Even Self is pleased to see it come again. See, she's smiling at it! I'm sorry, dear Prince, for being so bad today, and I'll never listen to Self any more. I really won't. And if it's true what Malignus says, that I'm a mean ungrateful little thing and the King's tired of me, I won't be mean any more. At least I'll try not."

"Do not trust to your own strength, Dilecta, for you are very weak. But the King loves you and will send you help whenever you ask him."

6

The King's Table

YOU might be sure that so generous a King and so kind a Father, would see that his subjects and his children were provided with all things necessary for them. But this is not saying enough. In a royal household we expect everything to be on a grand and imposing scale. We look for not merely a safe shelter from storms, and sufficient and suitable clothing for protection in all weathers, and rest and recreation after the labors of the day—but for these things in abundance. Above all, we look for a well-spread table, that none may go away hungry or disappointed; for food excellent in quality and unstinted in quantity, that all may grow up well and strong.

But would anyone expect a banquet every morning? Surely not. Even in royal nurseries this is not provided. Yet the good King did not think this was too much to prepare for the little guests at his table. He invited them, rich and poor, every day, and it was always a royal banquet that was made ready.

More than this. He himself set before the guests the costly food he had provided. Now, there were some folks who, thinking themselves wiser than the King, blamed him for this, saying that it was overmuch generosity and waste; that he made himself too cheap and would be treated with disrespect. Children of seven were too young to understand who he was and what he was giving them. They would not value the daily banquet which had cost him so much to prepare. They would not thank him. Nay, some, they said, would stay away because it was too much trouble to get up and make themselves fit to sit at his table.

But the King paid no attention to these wiseacres. He wanted the children round him. He knew that what he had made ready for them would make them strong, and good, and happy. He loved them and hoped the thought of his love would make them love him in return. So they were always welcome, and it was a beautiful sight to see him in the midst of the little white-robed throng.

One thing only he strictly required of all—the white robe. No one might come to his table without it, under pain of incurring his displeasure and dreadful punishment. A man had once dared to do so. He was driven out of the Banquet-Hall, and was never seen again. Near the hall was an ante-chamber where a white robe might be had by all who applied for it properly. Small stains on the robe did not prevent people from sitting down at the table. Still, the purer it was, the more welcome was the wearer, and the richer were the jewels with which the King was sure to adorn it. So the guests were advised to remove all spots as far as possible.

The King used to go amongst his guests with the presents he had for each. Those got the most and the best who had taken most trouble to get ready and who were most earnest in asking. If we ask for many things on our birthday, people think us greedy. The King never thought his visitors greedy. It was noticed that he was more pleased to give his good things than they were to get them. If ever he looked displeased or disappointed, it was when he was asked for nothing.

7

Dilecta Asks for a Change

D EAR Prince, I may always tell you everything and ask you anything, mayn't I?"

"Always, my child."

"Well, we are obliged, I know, to have Self with us in our huts. But I do so wish we could be without. I could get on quite well if I were alone. But Self is such a trouble to me. She wants me to go her way always. She doesn't care if it's a right or a wrong way so long as it's *her* way. And she's very hard to say 'No' to. And if I do say it, she gets so cross and sulky that the whole hut is turned upside down and is miserable to live in. I know you tell me that the more I give in to her the worse she will be, but one day last week I thought I would try to get peace by giving in to her a little bit. So I agreed with her in the morning that just for one day she should be first, and I would be the sub and do what she liked, unless, of course, it was wrong."

"How did the day go? Were you happy, and happy at night?"

"I can't say I was exactly, except just at first. Afterwards I was cross and miserable, and the more I gave in to her the horrider she got. And at night I was so vexed with her I wouldn't speak. Because, you know, she isn't fair. We agreed that she was not to want me to do anything wrong, but only things that didn't matter. Well, little by little, she did get me to do wrong things. Because, you see, I got so accustomed to saying 'Yes' to her about little finikin things she wanted, that when it was a big thing, even though it was wrong, I couldn't say 'No'. But I don't call that fair. And she's so cunning, too, coming to you when you're in trouble as if she was your friend, and advising you all wrong. I was feeling pretty bad yesterday with Rachel because she had trodden on my seeds just as they were coming up. Self was close by and whispered: 'Go and tread on hers this evening when there's nobody about, and see how she likes it. You'll feel ever so much better, and get rid of that nasty hot bubbling up inside that's like steam wanting to get out of the kettle'."

"Well?"

"I didn't do it because I had tried that way before, and though you're better for a minute, you're ever so much worse afterwards. But oh! I do get so tired. Do you think, dear Prince, the King would give me another Self—a nice one, you know, like poor old blind Bridget's, which gives no trouble? Whether it's a sunny day or a rainy one, she is always the same. I wish I could be like that."

"You will hardly believe it, Dilecta, but Bridget's Self was once so strong and fierce that you would have been afraid to vex such a companion. Especially when her blindness made her—that active woman, remember—so helpless and lonely. Self would come, and in a whining tone, pretending to pity her, say how hard it was on one so industrious and useful; how the King might have prevented it; how miserable she would be all the rest of her days, and so on."

"What did Bridget say?"

"That she had trusted the King always and trusted him still because she knew he loved her and would let nothing happen to her but what was for the best, as she would see some day. Self slunk away at this, but came back after a while, and always with the same teasing talk, pretending to be so sorry for the poor old thing in her trouble. But Bridget was a match for her Job's comforter. There was always the same patience, the same quiet trust in the King. Her peace lamp never went out. In the darkest night you may see it shining. Indeed, it is brightest when the wind is highest, and the night darkest, and the storm fiercest. If you could see, as I see, what is making ready in the Golden City for that humble, faithful servant of the King, you would never mistrust him, Dilecta, nor wish to mend his plans. Learn, too, from Bridget that the patient training of Self is rewarded at last, and what was once a very trying and even a dangerous comrade, may become a docile servant, a faithful friend.

"But you must do your part, remembering it is for you to take the lead. Treat Self quietly but firmly, and bear it patiently if she frets when you say 'No' to her. Do not wish you had a different Self, but train the one you have. There is plenty of good in her. (Dilecta looked up brightly.) I see improvement day by day. Cheer her up when she finds things hard. Remind her that where you go when you leave the Land of Exile, she will most certainly follow. So she must be a help, not a hindrance to you now. She must put up for a little while with things that are not to her liking, and comfort herself with the thought that if she behaves properly she shall have it all her own way by and by."

8

The King's Armory

THE children of the King's Household were taught, whilst they were quite small, who he was, and how much he loved them, and what they must do for him in return. They were taught, too, who Malignus was, how bad and cruel, how he hated them because they belonged to the King and were on their way to the Happy Land from which he was shut out. They knew they must not do as he told them, but they were not expected yet to go out and fight him as the soldiers of the Royal Army had to do. They were the King's children who would be made his soldiers later.

You may be surprised that the youngsters had to fight so soon. But trying out their strength is a thing children take to very readily, and the worse the war is, the younger are the soldiers who are called out to fight. The war between the King of the Golden City and Malignus, the traitor, was the deadliest you can imagine, because if a soldier did not come out victorious in the end, there was no trying again for him. So the children, girls as well as boys, had to be well taught, and taught young. It was wonderful how grandly some of them fought, how soon they got promoted, and how afraid of them their cunning old enemy came to be.

One day Dilecta was summoned to the King's Presence. She was so accustomed to go to him without ceremony, that she was rather frightened when the Prince Guardian told her she must kneel before him and listen very attentively to what he was going to say. Not without trembling she knelt down, the Prince standing reverently at her right hand.

"My child," said the King, "you are now old enough to be enrolled in my Army. Malignus is getting fiercer and more cunning, and what he cannot do by himself, he is going to employ others to do for him. You are beginning to listen to people who are not on my side, who are not afraid of breaking my laws, and who laugh at my servants who try to keep them. Besides these enemies without, you have Self always with you. She is growing fast and getting stronger and bolder. You must grow stronger, too, that you may be able to stand your ground and fight more bravely than you have done yet. I never send anyone to fight without providing a proper outfit. The Prince Guardian will take you to the Armory and get the equipment you need."

She was delighted and went off asking questions all the way.

The Armory was a wonderful place. There you could see the weapons of many a brave soldier who had laid aside his arms only when the fight was fought and won, and the palm of victory had been placed in his hand instead. The Prince Guardian took her in and out among the war trophies, and explained to her why they were treasured there. Here was the sword of St. Ignatius of Loyola, which he himself hung up in the House of God to show he was going to be henceforward a soldier of the King of kings alone. Over against it was the shield of St. Joan of Arc, the brave maid who fought for God and for her country.

Dilecta was immensely interested in all she saw—swords and shields, helmets and breastplates, and—shoes! She managed to make out the inscriptions:

On the sword—"FAITH."

On the shield—"TRUST IN GOD."

On the helmet—"PRAYER."

On the breastplate—"MISTRUST OF SELF."

On the shoes—"PATIENCE AND PERSEVERANCE."

"I think, Prince," she observed, "the shield and the breastplate are much the same."

"At least, they must always go together, Dilecta. 'Mistrust of Self' without 'Confidence in God' means discouragement, the beginning of all harm as you have discovered."

"What lots of helmets there are, more than I could count."

"Yes, for every victory is won by 'Prayer'. Never suppose you can fight all by yourself. Ask for help quickly, the moment you see your enemy."

"Look at all those shoes! Soldiers don't fight with them; what are they there for?"

"To show that 'Patience and Perseverance' in plodding on day after day, are necessary for every warrior. Opportunities of bringing the enemy down by a well-directed shot do not come every day nor does the need of meeting him with sword and shield in open fight. But every day there is the toilsome march, the same dull round of duty, the hardships inseparable from life at the front. It is the constant trudging of the weary feet that, more than anything else, brings a man to victory and reward."

So Dilecta was measured for her equipment and it was made to fit her exactly. And when all was ready, her Prince Guardian led her before the King and his Court. And she knelt down before them all and placed her little joined hands within the hands of the King, and promised to be a good soldier and faithful to him. And she was solemnly enrolled in the regular Army and given a mark by which everyone would know that she was now a soldier. That mark would be a disgrace should she turn out a traitor to the King, but a sign of distinction and glory if she remained faithful to him and fought his battles bravely.

Sword and shield and helmet and breastplate and shoes—he gave them all to her. Moreover, he promised that whatever help she wanted she should have the minute it was needed, if only she asked for it. At the end of the ceremony he gave her a little stroke on the cheek, not to hurt, but just to remind her that she must expect to suffer in his cause. Her three enemies would now be more than ever on the lookout for her, and like a soldier commanded to stand at "attention," she must be always on the alert.

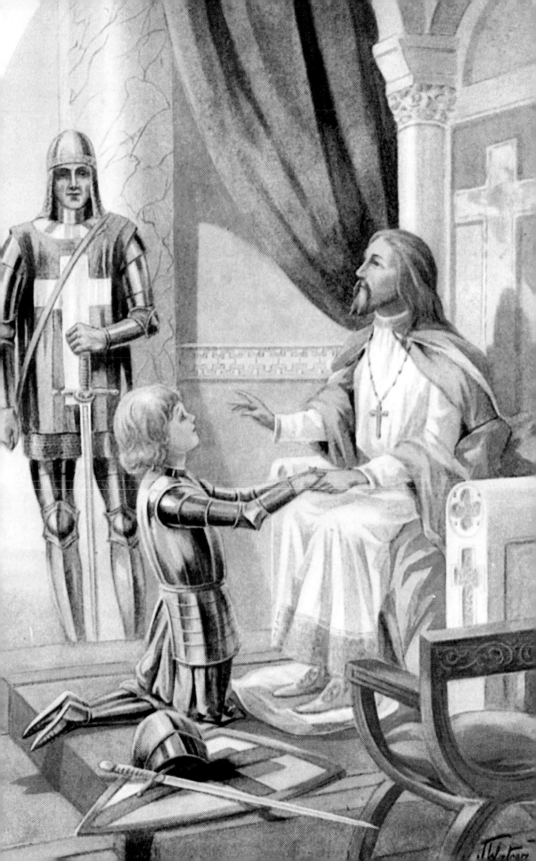

Two of these enemies, Malignus and Self, you know. They were like hand and glove and generally worked together. The King was speaking of the third enemy when he said Malignus had accomplices, or helpers who did for him what he could not do by himself. They were men, women, and even children, who could not wait for the good things of the Golden City. They said they wanted their good things *now*. "The time of our life," they said, "is short and tedious like the passing of a shadow. Come, therefore, and let us enjoy the good things that are present. Let us crown ourselves with roses before they be withered. Let us eat and drink, for tomorrow we die."

These people hated hard work and trouble of every sort. All they cared about was eating and drinking, dress and amusement, pleasure of every kind. They wanted to be as comfortable as money could make them; to be admired, and praised, and honored. They called themselves the "Jolly Ones" but their real name was "The Triflers."

"How shall I know them?" said Dilecta to her Prince Guardian. "I know Malignus and I know Self by what they say and do, but how shall I know the Triflers?"

"In the same way—by what they say, and what they do, and what they care about. All their talk is about the good things of the Land of Exile, and all their care is to please and amuse themselves. They do nothing to deserve the rewards of the King in the Golden City and have no fear of displeasing him. So far from trying to serve him, they do all they can to turn others from his service and to make them forsake the narrow, uphill way, which is the King's highway. They try to draw his servants into the broad way which belongs to Malignus and leads to his place. Beware of them. They are doing the work of their master, and if you go with them, you will grow like them, and will share their fate."

9

The King's Infirmary

I must tell you that the equipment which the King's soldiers received on the day of their enrollment in his army, though quite real, was not seen by others, nor even by themselves. Dilecta did not see her own, though she often felt it. She knew it belonged to her and she was almost eager for Malignus and those who helped him in his work to come along that she might try her new strength with them. It needed the reminder of her Prince Guardian that Prudence and Distrust of Self were part of her outfit, that shield and breastplate had *to be used* and her helmet kept ready for any danger, to prevent her from being rash.

When the soldiers of the King were overthrown in battle, two things happened—they were wounded, more or less severely, and their white robe was sullied. If the wound was slight, the robe was soiled only. If the wound was mortal, the white robe was not only soiled but spoilt, not only spoilt but lost altogether. In both cases the disaster came about through their own fault. Either they forgot to make use of their armor, or to call for the help they needed, or they fought in a half-hearted way, so that one of Malignus' well directed blows reached a weak spot and they were hurt.

Now, was any remedy provided by the King in these circumstances? Could anything be done to cleanse or recover the white robe if it had been soiled or lost? Could any mercy be shown to a traitor who—forsaking his Sovereign and going over to the enemy—had been mortally wounded? Surely not, you will say. But the kind King did not say so. In his Infirmary there were costly ointments that healed even mortal wounds. There were tender-handed, tender-hearted nurses who cared for the poor patients till they were well again. The white robe, too, could be cleansed or restored, the dark stains washed away. Who would not love and try to serve faithfully a King so good and forgiving?

One reason why the King's Infirmary was always full—stretchers with the wounded were continually being carried up the steps—was that his subjects did not take the daily food he had provided for them to keep them well and make them grow up healthy and strong. They took it sometimes but not as often as he wanted. Thus many of them were weak and sickly and gave Malignus a good chance when he came to attack them. Some came to the King's feast and saw him going round to the guests with his rich presents, or remedies for their complaints, but forgot to ask for anything when he came *to them*. Perhaps they did not understand that he really meant what he said when he called the food he had made ready their "daily bread." Perhaps they were not sure that he would really give them what they asked when he said, "Ask and you shall receive." Anyhow, to miss such a chance was very foolish of them, as they found out later.

10

The Little Maid in
an Idle Mood

A LTHOUGH the Prince Guardian was always within call whenever Dilecta was in need, and though no harm could come to her except through her own fault, he had warned her that she must watch over herself and not run into danger. More than once she had learned to her cost what comes of playing with fire.

You may have heard of the man who said to a thief: "There are two sides to my house, the inside and the outside. The inside I keep for myself, the outside I leave to you." This was the privilege of all in the Land of Exile —every man was complete master of his own house. There was no breaking in by force. The doors opened from the inside only: the windows were barred. No one could get in unless the owner let him in. Malignus could and did make himself extremely disagreeable from the outside. He could disturb, threaten, even alarm. He could come to the windows and coax and promise. But the smallest child knew that as long as the inmates said "No," he was kept outside. If people came to grief, then, it was their own fault.

One day as Dilecta stood in an idle mood at the little window of her hut, thinking what a trouble it was to have to learn lessons and do as she was told, and what a fine thing it would be to be a princess some day, she heard a soft knock at the door. I doubt if she would have heard it had she been going about her work, but as she was doing nothing, she did hear it.

Now, she knew that knock, and her Prince Guardian had told her never to listen to it but to go away from the door at once and get to work. She heard the Prince call to her, but instead of listening to him, she thought she would open the door ever so little and just peep out to see what was there. She lifted the latch, and—straightway a great ugly foot was thrust in, and a lean hand came round the door and tried to catch her. Oh, how frightened she was!

"Prince! Prince!" she cried, "come quick, I can't hold the door, he's pushing so hard!"

At once the Prince was at her side. But it was no easy matter to get the hand and the foot out again. When at last this was done the Prince Guardian said:

"You have done wrong, my child. Had you not called out at once, Malignus would have got right in and hurt you dreadfully, and the King would have been angry. You must tell him at once how sorry you are."

She met the King soon after in the wood and told him what she had done, and when he saw that she was sorry, he forgave her.

But next time he came to the little hut and she knelt at his feet and looked into his face, she saw it was not quite the same as usual. It was grave. And he did not smile nor stroke her hair. He seemed sad.

"Dear King," she said, "why don't you speak to me today? Is it because I was naughty last week? But you forgave me, didn't you?"

"I forgave you, Dilecta," he said. "I will always forgive you when you are sorry and come to me. But I want you to know that just because I love you so much I am sad when you disobey me. When you hurt me you hurt yourself too, and it is this that makes me sad. Though I forgive you, you have a debt of punishment to pay when you do wrong. It must all be paid before you can be let into the Golden City. I want to have you there soon, but you will have to wait outside until you have paid the debt."

"How can I pay it, dear King?"

"By whatever you do to please me, even by things you like to do, and by bearing patiently things you do not like—cold and hunger, hard work, disappointments and cross words, the struggle with yourself when temptation comes and you want to be idle or disobedient, or unkind. Whenever you try to overcome Self, you are paying off your debt. It is because I want you to have it all paid before I take you away from the Land of Exile, that I let troubles come to you here. They are the money I give you to pay with. Remember this, and you will not be impatient. Know that I send them because I love you. You saw I was grave and silent today when I came into your hut. Think that you deserved it, that it will help you to pay what you owe, and you will not be discouraged or sad. Whenever I come to you I come to help, even when I do not speak much or show all the love that is in my heart. On these days I am giving those I love the money with which they can pay their debts."

She looked up into his face through her tears, and said softly as she took him to the door: "Have I paid some of my debt today?"

11

The Broad Road

DILECTA'S daily life and duties were not, as we have seen, of a very exciting kind. But one thing she and the little folk of the neighboring villages did look forward to—the yearly fair or circus. Months beforehand, the wares, the shows, the sports, the dresses to be worn on the occasion, were the main subjects of conversation.

One year there was to be something quite new and thrilling. No one exactly knew what, but a band of strolling players had been announced, whose performance was to be quite the sensation of the week. The youngsters were brimful of joyful expectation, but some of the elders shook their heads, and more than one father and mother forbade their children to go to the play in the evening.

Her Prince Guardian would not hear of Dilecta being present. It was a woeful disappointment to have to give up the treat on which she had set her heart, and she told him so in terms more precise, perhaps, than respectful:

"Am I never to enjoy myself?" she said tearfully. "Girls ever so much younger than I am are going. Prince, you are always telling me to do hard things: you don't mind how much it hurts."

"My little sister," he answered tenderly, "you will know some day how much I care for you and how glad I am to see you happy. Except to keep you from harm, I would never ask you to go against your likes and dislikes. There will be plenty of other amusements, but this show I cannot approve. We will go together to the fair, stay till 8, and then come away."

"Daisy is going and she will stay all the time."

"Daisy must answer for herself. As your guardian I am bound to caution you against what would be bad *for you.*"

Dilecta pouted. She knew he was right. Her conscience was always on his side, whichever way her likings went. But she would not give in and went about cross all day. She was cross with the girls she met; cross with her poor blind friend; cross even with the goat that came for its usual petting.

The night before the fair opened she was standing at the door of her hut, the Prince Guardian on one side, Self, as usual, on the other.

"Dilecta," he said gravely, "I am going to the King and am to take your answer to him. You know he speaks to you through me. Are you going to disappoint him?"

"The King comes to me the day after tomorrow. I will explain to him then."

"Are you going, child, to run such risk? If you do what will make him angry with you, you can hope for no visit from him next day. And how do you know you will have another day? Every hour, children younger than you are being called for by the King. They are brought through the Dark Valley to stand before him to hear their sentence. If they were his friends when they set out on that last journey, they will be his friends always. But if they were not . . . oh, my child, take care, take care!"

She hesitated still, looked up, and saw his face turned in the direction of the Golden City with a look of intense supplication. She felt he was praying for her, and the hardness of her heart gave way. A moment of fierce struggle . . . and the battle was won! Falling on her knees she cried: "Forgive me, Prince, I am sorry. Tell the King I will not go!"

T he theater was a great tent set up in the middle of a field. Round the entrance, hung with staring bills and gaudy flags, thronged the children in admiring groups. They had never seen anything like it before and longed to go inside.

Among the loiterers was a girl named Daisy who had managed to get together a certain number of followers. Older and better off than the rest, she had brought them so completely under her power, that they were afraid to contradict her in anything. Her word was law, and because she gave them treats, they flattered and obeyed her like a troop of slaves even when they knew she was in the wrong.

Now, Daisy and her "set," as they were called, had tried to gain over Dilecta to their party, but the Prince Guardian of the child had succeeded hitherto in keeping his little charge aloof from both the leader and her followers.

Here I must stop for a moment to tell you of something that has been mentioned several times—a certain broad road of the Land of Exile, which passed through every city, village and hamlet, however lowly and retired. All that Dilecta and the village children knew about it was that it began a long way off and led downward to a great distance, further than any of them had ever been. No one knew where it stopped, because after winding in and out as far almost as the eye could follow, it suddenly turned and was lost to sight.

This road, not of hard flint or gravel, but of beautiful, soft, springy grass, was shaded by tall trees, and lined on both sides by shrubs and flowers, with fruit trees here and there, and comfortable lounges where one could rest. It was more like a park or pleasure-ground than a highway, for the delicious fruits hung within reach of the passersby who could help themselves to any that looked inviting.

The road was always thronged with the careless and the gay of every age and class. Old and young, great folks of the fashionable world in elegant attire, rustics smart and showy in their Sunday best, sauntered along, or lay lazily on the grass, seeking by various devices to kill time and banish anything like disquieting thoughts. Sometimes a band came along, and then the pleasure seekers—one could hardly call them travelers—joined in a dance. Roses in abundance grew by the wayside. These the girls would pluck and twine in their hair, though it was well known that little poisonous snakes often hid under the shrubs and stung badly when disturbed. No one seemed to learn by experience and every one was sure that no harm would happen, at least *to her*.

Merrymaking was the business of life on this flowery path, which was the favorite resort of Daisy and her friends. Dilecta used to watch them from the high bank above, and as the shouts of laughter rose, she wished at times that she might join them on that pleasant road.

"Dear Prince," she said one day, "don't you like to see me enjoy myself with others?"

"My child, I am always glad to see you merry, but not on the broad road. Have you never noticed that some of these revelers come back in the evening with their white robes soiled and their faces discontented and sad?"

Hitherto Dilecta had seldom met "the set," but the fair had united all the children of the place in a common interest, and she was beginning to mix freely with all and talk over the pleasures they were expecting. It had come out that she was not going to the play in the evening, and there was much discussion among "the set" as to the whys and wherefores of so extraordinary a decision.

"Daisy says we are all to be there," said one of them. "She has made up a party who are to go with her and Flos is to be with us." (I expect you have forgotten that "Dilecta" was the King's name for the child he had met in the wood and had made his little favorite. To everyone else, except the Prince Guardian, she was "Flos.")

"As to leaving before the fun begins," said Daisy, who was vexed at being thwarted by one so much younger than herself, "it's simply absurd and we won't stand such nonsense. She'll have to change her mind, that's all."

It happened that as Daisy, surrounded by her party, was watching the final preparations for the various entertainments to be provided, she spied Dilecta in the distance on her way home. A sign from their leader, and the whole troop was in pursuit. In a few minutes they were back with their prisoner.

"Why won't you go to the play?" said one.

"It will be the best part of the day," cried another.

"I wouldn't miss it for anything," broke in a third.

"I *am* going," Dilecta replied.

"But you're leaving at 8. Why on earth do you go so soon, the best things don't come off till night."

"I have to leave at 8."

"But why, why?" they cried impatiently.

"Oh! I know," said Daisy with a sneer. "It's because she thinks herself so much better than we are that she won't go anywhere in our company. It's a mighty fine thing to be a saint." And she folded her hands and put on a solemn look which sent them all into fits of laughter.

"I don't think myself better, and I'm not a saint," exclaimed Dilecta, turning crimson.

"Then show you're not, and do as we do," was the cry.

"Stand back, then, and I'll show you."

They fell away on either side, and . . like a shot she had darted through the ring and was well on her way home before they had recovered from their surprise.

There was no attempt at pursuit for she was well known as the fleetest runner far and near. But, though outwitted, they would not acknowledge defeat.

"Did you notice how red she got when Daisy called her a saint?" said one.

"Yes," answered another, "we will have her yet."

12

The Fair

THERE was the bustle and excitement usual at a fair. Cries of many kinds, music and laughter, were heard on every side. Children in holiday dress went from one attraction to another, making themselves giddy and sick on merry-go-rounds, screaming with delight round a cage of traveling monkeys, venturing near a poor bear that was dragged about by a chain and made to do tricks that did not amuse him in the least. Here were men and women, dark-skinned and gypsy-looking, selling all kinds of jewelry of wonderful brilliance and cheapness. Over there a man was displaying books with fascinating titles and pictures.

Dilecta went about with the swarm of children, now in one group, now in another, enjoying everything. She was sad though, as the day wore on, to think she must not stay for the great event of the evening, and somewhat frightened at the possibility of not being able to get away. She had come to know her weakness, and was afraid of herself. Many a time that afternoon she turned to the strong friend at her side, and begged him to be at hand when the time for the struggle came.

Wandering about, and coming near to the gay book stall, she felt herself gently drawn to one side, as though there were unseen danger near. What could it be? There was only the man crying his goods and inviting customers. Suddenly she caught sight of one who was no stranger. Indeed, he had shown himself more than usually meddlesome of late. Creeping about among the books, looking into them here and there, passing over some, pausing over others, was . . . Malignus!

"What is he doing there?" she asked the Prince Guardian.

"Minding his own business. Some of those books belong to him. He helped the men and women who wrote them, and he is putting his mark into them. They will do his work, and he will be near by when boys and girls take them up to get amusement out of them."

You must have found out by this time that Malignus had many ways of harming the subjects of the King. By one or other of his tricks he managed to hurt even the wary ones at times. But those were silly who let themselves be caught over and over again in the same traps. For they knew how to recognize him when he came their way. "How?" you will ask. "He was not always visible—indeed, he preferred darkness to light for working purposes—how could people know he was about?"

There were certain signs. Something whirls past you on a country road. You know it must be a motor by the noise and fluster with which it comes rushing upon you out of nowhere, by the haste with which sensible people get out of its way, by the cloud of dust it raises, and the horrid smell it leaves behind. Wherever Malignus went, the poisoned atmosphere, and a sudden haze which caused confusion and trouble, showed he was somewhere near. Wise persons came to note these signs and were on their guard when they appeared.

He would come up with a smile and offer bad sweets, sparkling with sugar, to little children. He would sprinkle poisonous powders into books, so that readers were injured for life, or killed outright by using them. Sometimes he laid snares to trip people up. He would fight with children himself, or get their companions to do his work for him. But he was always prowling about to see what harm his soft whispered words or his cruel blows could do.

Often enough, especially when dealing with those who wanted to be the King's faithful soldiers, he would be content with frightening them, making them think that they were breaking the King's laws when they were not. He used to rub his hands with satisfaction if he had made a little child cry. He liked to disappoint a child by promising something he never meant to give, or that would hurt if it was given. You will think it disgraceful that one so strong and clever should not be ashamed to fight with a child. It was disgraceful. But cowards are not easily ashamed. And if ever there was a coward, it was Malignus. An infant could frighten him away. A big dog that has been hurt by a stone thrown at it, may be driven away by a little child simply stooping as if to pick up a stone. Malignus was like that. At the mere sound of the King's name on the lips of a babe, he would tremble like a leaf.

But we must get back to the fair.

Dilecta saw the Prince Guardians following their little charges from one scene of attraction to another, time after time preventing them from coming to grief in one or other of the many ways a fair provides.

It was nearly 8 o'clock when, making her way through a crowd of children who were watching with frantic expressions of delight the antics of some performing monkeys, she came upon two of "the set," bedecked with rings, necklaces, and other trinkets which Daisy had bought them. They were peering about as if in search of some one. As soon as they caught sight of her, they cried to others behind: "Here she is!" and in a moment she was a prisoner.

"It's no good, Flos, you really must stay. It's going to be lovely and so exciting—a real shipwreck in the first scene."

"Don't press her," exclaimed a mocking voice. "Saints never go to shipwrecks; it wouldn't be right."

Dilecta flushed up. "I told you I wasn't a saint, but I'm not going to stay all the same."

"We don't want you to go to anything but the first scene. You've always wanted so much to see the sea. Well, this is just as good; a real storm and waves all moving, and thunder and lightning, and the ship going down, and all the people jumping into the water and trying to get to the boats."

By this time they had got her to the door, and the crowd was closing in behind them. They noticed she did not struggle as at first, and one of them thought she said: "Well, only for the first scene, then."

"We've got such a lovely place," said Daisy, "and, oh! Flos, you do look nice."

She was jammed in between two jailers. The place was filling fast, filling to suffocation.

The clock struck 8. All eyes were fixed on the screen.

"Dilecta," said the Prince Guardian, "you should not be here. Come with me!"

"How can I? They are going to begin and I can't get out."

"Come with me!"

"Help me, then, oh, help me!"

There was a stir just behind her; a woman had fainted and was being carried out. Dilecta followed. How, she could never tell. But in a few minutes the cool air was blowing on her face. The fair was left behind, and she was on her way home.

That night she was surprised to find the light of the Peace lamp so bright. She had missed the treat on which she had counted so long, but she had found a happiness never felt before, more satisfying by far than any pleasure the play could have given. "It will be over now," she thought, as after a short sleep she woke and began to think how nearly she had been caught in the trap laid for her, and how much she owed to the faithful friend who had warned and saved her.

She could not go to sleep again. So she got up and went to the window. It was about midnight. No stars were out. The night was still except for the bursting now and then of a rocket from the gala scene of the fair.

Suddenly, there shot up into the sky a red flare, then another, and another, and she fancied she heard cries. For a few moments the heavens were lit up in the direction of the fair; then the flames sank lower and lower, and all was still again. Her heart beat violently. She turned to the Prince Guardian at her side:

"What is this? What does it mean?"

"It means, Dilecta, that a fire has broken out at the playhouse, and that many of those who went there for amusement are now passing through the Dark Valley on their way to the Land whence there is no return."

Next morning the news went abroad that in the midst of the performance, the theater, hastily put together, had caught fire. A panic followed, and many of the sightseers in the rush to the one door by which they could get out, had perished. Daisy and her companions, with one exception, were among the victims.

When Dilecta met the King that day her heart was full of many thoughts. She threw herself at his feet to thank him for her deliverance from the terrible fate that had befallen others. And he said:

"Learn to trust me always. Believe that my commandments are meant to keep you from harm. Say now what all in the

Happy Land say in transports of joy and thankfulness as they look back upon my dealings with them in the Land of Exile:

"He hath done all things well!"

13

The Little Maid Learns
Some Lessons

DILECTA was getting wiser and braver. She was beginning to notice that she was not happier when she was thinking only of pleasing herself. Just at first, perhaps, there was a little pleasure, but it soon passed and in its place came disappointment and sadness which made her snappish and disagreeable to others. It was a good thing that she found this out, for it helped her to say "No" to Self when she had to choose between what was wrong but tempting and what was right but hard.

Not that she always chose the right now. Oh, dear no! Often and often Self got what she wanted, and the Prince Guardian had to turn away disappointed because Dilecta would not listen to his warning voice.

Before she did anything wrong, Malignus used to tell her that it was only a little thing; it really didn't matter much; the King would not be very angry nor shut her out of the Golden City. She could be sorry directly after and he would forgive her. On the other hand, her Prince Guardian checked her, saying little things do matter, and if she were to get into the way of disobeying the King in small things, she might some day break his law in a big thing and make him very angry with her.

When in spite of this warning she did wrong to please herself—see what happened. The Wicked One who had told her it was only a trifle which the King would not mind, now turned upon her and called her an ungrateful little wretch. The King could not love her, he said, and it was not true to tell him she was sorry. She had told him so hundreds of times and made him fine promises again and again. He was tired of her. It was no use trying any more to please him; she might as well give it up and enjoy herself.

And her Prince Guardian, what did he say when she had refused his advice and made herself miserable? Did he reproach her sharply and say it was no use trying?

"My child," he said gently, "you did wrong just now by not listening to me. Do not do more wrong by listening to Malignus, who wants to make you discouraged and unhappy. Our dear King is very kind, very forgiving. He knows his little Dilecta really wants to love and please him, but that she is very weak. Tell him now that you are sorry. As soon as you see that you are doing what he does not like, stop doing it. Tell him you are sorry you began to do it, and he will forgive you. Then go on as before. Try again as if you had never saddened him. Do this as often as you fall into any fault. Get up at once as you would if your foot slipped in crossing a road. You would not sit there crying till a motor came and drove over you. But you would jump up at once and go on as before, very little the worse for your tumble, perhaps even, the better for it because it would make you more careful in the future."

Many and many a time had Dilecta to recall this lesson. It is not so easy to learn as you might think. Her instructors often found her very trying. She was obstinate, careless, and oh! she was idle. The little wild colt did not like being put into harness and made to work. When those who had charge of her reproved her, she did not consider that they were in the King's place and bound to find fault when she disobeyed his commands and behaved in a way unbefitting one who was to be a princess in his Court. She would think they disliked her, and would answer back, or, worse still, sulk, so that it was very hard for them to know how to train her. Then, when the naughty fit was over and she was sorry, she felt inclined to pout and say she would never be fit to be a princess. She fought against this discouragement and tried to do as her Prince Guardian had told her, but it was hard.

14

What the King Loved
in the Little Maid

I have told you some of the faults of the little maid; it is only fair that I should tell you her good points, too. She was very truthful. I believe it was this that chiefly charmed the King. He was himself so frank and true, that he could not do with people whose goodness was mere presence; who were diligent only when they were watched; who believed that certain persons held his place, yet deceived them as soon as their backs were turned. It was because Dilecta was straightforward that he loved her. He had told her from the first that he wanted to know all about herself—her joys, troubles, struggles, efforts—everything. She used to tell him, especially when he came into her hut where they were so quiet together, all that had happened since he was there last, all that was in her mind. And he could always trust her to tell the truth. Everything interested him, every little ache and pain, every bit of improvement in the hut, every hard lesson she had tried to learn to please him.

One day he had been told that she had shown herself more than usually unruly and had stamped her foot at one of her instructors.

"Yes," she said, "I did."

"And you never told me about it?" His kind eyes looked into hers. "Tell me about it now," he said.

"I wanted to go and see some pictures, and they wouldn't let me, because they said they were not fit for a princess to see.

So I got cross. And when my sums wouldn't come right I got crosser and crosser, and at night when I had to do an exercise over again, I stamped my foot. But I did try all day, indeed I did. I wanted to stamp in the morning, but I didn't and when the sums went wrong, and I didn't. But at night I did stamp, so it's all no good and it's no use my trying."

She looked pitifully into his face, but he was smiling.

"And you tried all day?" he said.

"Yes."

"And just at night you broke down?"

"Yes."

"And do you think I am going to be angry or disappointed when you fought for me all day and just for a moment lost ground? My child, you have been a brave little soldier and deserve, not blame but reward. You must go on trying and some day I shall be proud of you."

She looked up again, and *she* was smiling now. "Do you want me, dear King, to tell you always about my bad days? I thought you only cared to hear about nice things that I do to please you."

"Fighting days, Dilecta, are not bad days, even when you break down now and then. I am with my soldiers when they fall as well as when they fight. When they fall I pity them and help them up, and when they are badly hurt I dress their wounds myself. Be sorry at once when you have given way before the enemy. Trust in me and my help. You will grow stronger each time you try. It is to help you to grow strong that I come to you often. By yourself you are very weak, but you and I together are more than a match for the enemy."

15

How the King Found the Little Maid Sad One Day

———————————————

ON one of his visits the King found the little maid sad and he wanted to know the reason. At first she was ashamed to say what was in her mind, but it came out at last.

"Dear King, I thought you said you loved me with all your heart?"

"I did, Dilecta. I never do anything by halves."

"But you love others, too, and there will be other princesses in the Golden City besides me?"

"You were sitting in the warm sunshine this morning, Dilecta. Did you grudge his warmth to your friends who were sitting round you?"

"Oh, no, there was enough for us all. And besides, I was glad they were happy, too."

"And I am glad to see those I love happy. If you love me you will love all whom I love. My love is like the sunshine; it is for all my people, and at the same time it is all for my little Dilecta as if it were for her alone. She must not be selfish. She must love all who are dear to me and love them for my sake. And because they have places in the Golden City and I am waiting for them there, she must try to help them all she can."

"Are there many princesses who love you more than I do?" she asked shyly.

The King smiled. "Your love is not very strong as yet," he said, "but I care for it very much and each time I come to you I make it stronger."

"Tell me about those who love you more than I do."

"There is a child," he replied, "who never refuses me anything I ask of her, and is more afraid of displeasing or disappointing me than of any pain to herself. She often tells me she wants to love me as I have never yet been loved."

"I shall never be able to say that," said Dilecta sadly.

"But you may say it," he answered. "The love of every heart is different, and because I love all, I want the love of all. Your love, Dilecta, is not quite like any other. If you do not give it to me I shall never have it from anyone else. So you may well want to love me as I have never yet been loved."

"Tell me how people—how *I* may come to love you very dearly. I should like to give you my very own love, dear King, if you care to have it."

"Try to learn about me," he said. "Think often how I have loved you and suffered for you, how I want to be with you here on the way to the Golden City, and to make you happy there with me. And try to be like me. I am kind to all, even to those who are not kind to me and who do not love me. There are many to whom I have given all they have, yet they never thank me nor try to please me.

"All in the Golden City are like me. There is no envy among them. They all love one another, and are glad because they see how much I love them, everyone. Some are higher and more beautiful and more loved by me than others, because they have loved me more. But all are quite content and happy, for there is no selfishness in that bright land where they only want what I want. If you will try to be like them now, Dilecta, you shall be like them and with them some day."

"Dear King, I will try."

Soon after this she had a chance to show him whether her promises were mere words, or something better. An unkind story had been told about her, and it wasn't true. It made her feel very hot and angry and she said to herself: "I know what I will do to vex that mischiefmaker. *I* can make mischief, too. I will just go and tell what was said to me last week and Dora will find herself in hot water." And she rubbed her hands at the thought.

But then another thought came. What would the King say? Would this be doing as he had taught her? Would this be loving and helping all whom he loved? A great struggle began. She did so want to pay back and say the spiteful words. And yet she wanted to please the King. Her Prince Guardian came to her help. He told her that if the unkind words were said, there would be just a little pleasure, for a minute perhaps—and then *such pain*. To think she could not make this little sacrifice for the King! To think this was her return to him whom, after all, she did love! But if she gained a victory over herself, how pleased he would be. She would have this little present ready for him next time he came.

At last the battle was over—and won! To be like the King who was gentle and kind even to those who did not love him, she would be kind, too. Because she loved him, she would not say the words that would make him sad.

What a reward she had next time he came to see her! She thought she had never seen his smile so bright as she stood at the door and let him in.

16

The Golden City

T ELL me, dear King, something about the Golden City," said the little maid one day. "I think sometimes the Palace will be too grand for me. You see I'm not used to grand things."

"Remember, Dilecta, that it is your own Country to which you are going, and that the Palace will be your Home."

"I've never had a home here. But I've heard about other people's homes. They've had a kind father and mother, and brothers and sisters, and friends. And lovely houses, and gardens, and horses, and dogs, and birds, and books . . . oh! such a lot of things that I've never had. It makes me long to have them. I wonder if it's wrong. I know it makes me unhappy."

"My child, you are meant to be happy, and you can never long enough for the things that will make you happy. But I will tell you a secret, Dilecta. All the delightful things that make up home, here in the Land of Exile, never quite satisfy those who have them. Those who have most want more. If anyone could have all there is to have, he would still wish for something different and better. And even if he could be satisfied for a little while, he would soon have to leave everything. Every day you see people going down into the Dark Valley that lies round the Land of Exile, and setting out, with nothing at all in their hands of all they had here, for a Land they will never leave."

"Do they all get safe to the Golden City?"

"Not all. They are sent here for a short time only, with a work to do. When that work is done, or the end of time for doing it is come, they are taken hence. Now, many of these exiles forget that they are in exile and try to make themselves at home *here*. They neglect the task they were set to do, get together whatever will make them comfortable, and think of nothing but enjoying themselves."

"Do they know when the King will send for them?"

"No one knows. Their time may be long or it may be short. They may have warning. They may have none. Suddenly, at cockcrow, in the noontide heat, at eventide, in the quiet of night, or in the midst of noisy pleasures, the call may come. All must be found watching, for at what hour they think not, their Lord will come."

"I think it's very silly of them not to get on with their work, because if they don't, it mightn't be ready when the King sends for them. What would happen then?"

"If they have been bad servants and neglected the King's service altogether, he has to banish them from his sight and send them away into a terrible exile which they will never leave. All that he had made ready for them in his Palace which was to be their Home, they will never have. All the love and the joy and the happiness their hearts long for, will never be theirs because it is only to be found where the King is, in the Golden City, and they have made themselves unworthy to be with him."

"Then it's better not to have too many nice things here, if people get too fond of them?"

"It is safer and better. You are poor, Dilecta. You have not many of what are called the 'good things' of the Land of Exile. But I have more than you have ever wished for, waiting for you. It shall all be yours some day."

"Dear King, there is something I should like . . . oh! so very much. But . . . but . . . I don't think even you could give it to me. You couldn't have *a mother* waiting for me . . . could you?"

"My child, I knew you were going to ask me that. Yes, there is a mother longing and waiting for you, loving you as only a mother can love, and ready to help you always."

"And are there brothers and sisters, too? I have never had anyone to play with."

"All you can wish for or think of is there—companions and friends, joy and love on every side. Your eyes have never seen, your ears have never heard what I have ready for those who love me."

The King was looking fixedly into a far distance. Her eyes tried to follow his gaze. She saw that he was seeing all he spoke of. Presently she said timidly:

"If I could see only just once what you see, I don't think I should ever want to go down the Broad Road again."

He was silent for a moment, as if considering. Then, looking down on the earnest, pleading face, he said:

"You cannot see now as you will see one day. But because you have prayed so hard, you shall have something that will show you more clearly the things you long to see. You know of them already. It is because you know of them that your Prince Guardian and your teachers have been able to train you. What you ask, what I will give you, is a closer, clearer view of these things. This gift is very precious. Take care of it and keep it bright. The more you use it the brighter it will become. It will serve you right up to the end of the Dark Valley, to the Gates of the Golden City."

He was gone. But his promise filled her heart with joyful expectation. Something "very precious," therefore to be well guarded. Something to be "kept bright" and to be "well used" . . . what could the gift be?

The rest of that day Dilecta was kept hard at work. Rushes for her baskets had to be got and steeped in water, and a little cake taken to poor blind Bridget. Her thoughts ran continually on the King's gift and what it would show her, but she tried to do well what she had to do, and to wait patiently, though she knew that by the time she got back to her hut there would not be much light to see anything.

The sun had set when she lifted the latch and looked round. The Peace lamp was lighting up the little place as usual with its quiet glow, and everything seemed as she had left it. The King's present, then, had not come yet. Stay! there was something on her little stool, a small telescope with a word on it in shining, golden letters—"FAITH." She took it to the window and put it to her eyes. Instantly there streamed from it a strong, steady brilliance which shot up like a searchlight into the heavens. And she herself was . . . where? Far, far away from the mud walls of her hut, her little hard couch, the scenes of her daily life; far away in a new and wonderful world of sights and sounds of which she had never so much as dreamed.

Before her rose a City of pure gold, bright as crystal. Its walls and very foundations were precious stones. Its twelve gates were twelve pearls, one great pearl to each gate. Its streets pure gold, as clear as transparent glass. Through the midst flowed a river of water clear as crystal, and on each bank grew a tree of wondrous fruits. The City had neither sun nor moon to shine in it, yet there was no night there.

Upon a Great White Throne, a throne of light, was One sitting, King of kings and Lord of lords, having on his head a crown of gold. And round the Throne, clothed in white robes, with palms in their hands, stood thousands of thousands, of all nations, and tribes and peoples, and tongues. And they cast their crowns of gold before the Throne, and their voices went up in songs of praise and thanksgiving, as the noise of many waters and as the voice of harpers harping upon their harps. For them there was no more hunger nor thirst, neither did the sun fall on them nor any heat. All tears were wiped from their eyes; and death was no more, nor mourning, nor crying, nor sorrow, any more, for the former things were passed away. "Let us be glad and rejoice," they sang. "Give praise to our King all ye his servants, and you that fear him, little and great."

And—glorious above all that glorious throng—appeared a Woman clothed with the sun, the moon under her feet, and on her head a crown of twelve stars.

Long did Dilecta stand that night, her glass turned to the skies, seeing and hearing far beyond the measureless regions of space around. Yes, hearing as well as seeing. Her telescope bore the five golden letters—"FAITH," and by its power she could not only see into the depths of the Golden City, but could hear its songs of joy.

You may think how she prized that glass of hers. True, the visions it showed were dimmed because of her weak sight and the mists of the Land of Exile. But she knew what it showed was true, more real than the sights and sounds of her daily life. When these weighed heavily upon her, when she was weary of being an exile in the "Valley of Tears," she would take up the King's matchless gift, and . . . in an instant be far away . . . in the Land, the City, the Palace, the Home, it opened out to her. Day by day the lens became clearer, the songs nearer and sweeter, the glance of that star-crowned Queen and Mother, brighter, and the desire of her own eager heart stronger, to see—not as now, hidden and in disguise—but face to face, the King of kings and Lord of lords, who being the brightness of that glorious City, had loved and chosen . . . *her.*

17

The Land of Weary Waiting

THE King had told Dilecta that besides the Golden City, her glass would show her other things. Turned towards the ground, it showed something very different. But she was not to turn it this way often, only when Malignus, or the Triflers, or Self, pressed her very hard and she was afraid of giving in to them. Then she would find it useful. Set upon suddenly one day by Malignus and Self, she did use it in this way, and in an instant its light pierced the hard crust of the earth beneath her feet. The terrible things she saw helped her at once, sent Malignus flying off at full speed, and set her feet firmly on the King's side in the battle. Indeed, what she saw that day so frightened her that she never forgot it and hardly ever had to turn her glass that way again.

If she held the glass midway between heaven and earth, Dilecta saw in this middle distance a strange sad land, called the Land of Weary Waiting. Here were gathered together a multitude of the King's friends, looking wistfully towards the Golden City. Now and then they could catch a note of its songs. Some of them even thought they could see its gates of pearl.

Why were they there? Because they owed debts to the King which must be paid before they could be set free and go to him. These debts might have been paid off in the Land of Exile had the debtors been wise enough to see to this. But they were not, so they had to wait and wait and pay their debts by dreadful pain, because they had no other money now to pay with.

It was a land of sadness because of the waiting and the pain, but a land of hope, too, because the poor prisoners knew their names were written in the Book of Life and so they were sure of their places in the Golden City.

I will try to explain to you what their pain was like.

Have you ever been in a hothouse where the heat was so suffocating that you felt unless you could get directly to the door and the fresh air outside, you would die? Well, one and all—the King's enemies as well as his friends—feel like that, the moment the Land of Exile is left behind. The sight of the King in his beauty, the enjoyment of being with him—this is the very breath of their life; without it, they must lie gasping in agony. So they all rush towards him as soon as ever the Dark Valley is passed, and if anything stops them even for a second, they fall back in suffocating pain.

Some—his enemies—see him for an instant, and then have to be sent away from him for ever, to bear that awful agony . . . always, always.

Others—his friends—have to be sent away, too, to bear that terrible pain until their debts are paid.

With pitying, tearful eyes Dilecta watched them, and turning to her Prince Guardian, asked if she could help them. He showed her that she could. By doing her lessons and daily work for the King, by bearing her daily troubles bravely to please him, by being kind for his sake to all whom he loved, she was saving up money to pay her debts when she, too, would come to the prison-place. Now, if she liked, she could give some of her savings to the poor prisoners who could not help themselves. Thus she could pay their debts for them.

Oh, how glad she was to hear this! From that time she came to be quite a little friend to these poor friends of the King. She saved all she could; and even went without things she liked that she might have more to send them. Her Prince Guardian who took her messages and her gifts, told her how they watched for his coming and how grateful they were to her for what she sent. The King, too, was grateful to her, for he did so want to have them with him soon. And he told Dilecta that when it was her turn to go to the place of weary waiting, he would remember that she had been kind to others. And all those whom she had helped into the Golden City would come to her help just in the same measure as she had come to theirs.

You see, then, what a good thing it was that Dilecta asked the King so earnestly that day that she might see the things Faith could show her. Because she wanted this and prayed for it, he sent her that wonderful glass. He told her she must prize it as the most precious of his gifts. Should she be so unhappy as to lose the others, Faith could bring them back, but if Faith itself were lost, it was very, very hard to get it again.

18

Brave Love

HOW many things the King taught the little maid in those visits of his—and what happy times they had together! She would sit on the mud floor at his feet, or on the bench by his side and tell him all that was in her heart, for he liked to hear everything, everything. She loved him so much now that her old selfishness grew less every day. She had come to care for what he loved, and not only for presents and what pleased herself. She often asked him what she could do for him, even at her own cost; how she could help those who were dear to him and who were hungry or cold or in trouble. Though she was poor herself, she would save up her pennies to get something warm for the King's friends who were poorer still. He had told her that whatever she did for his friends he would take as done to himself. Sometimes she would do quite hard things that she might hear him say: "You did it unto me." Her love, you see, was getting to be a brave love.

One morning a strange thing happened when he came to see her. She felt as if she did not care to see him, did not want the trouble of getting ready for him. She felt cross and miserable, tired of everything; tired of trying to please him. Oh, was the old sad time coming back when she had grown careless and left him alone when he came? She began to wonder whether it was her own fault this time, but she could not remember anything in particular that would make her afraid to meet the King. And yet she was afraid.

He came, and she had nothing to say to him. Was he angry with her, for he did not say much either? She told him she was glad to see him and things like that, but she felt as if she did not mean what she said. Altogether she felt strange and sad, and when he took his leave, there was no eagerness in her invitation to come again.

The next time he came, it was the same, and the next, and the next. At last she said to him:

"Dear King, what is the matter? Why are you so different with me now? Are you displeased with me?"

He looked at her lovingly and said: "No, Dilecta, I am not displeased. But you have asked me to teach you how to love me like those who love me best, not for my gifts but for myself. I am teaching you now. When I first came to you, you were always looking out for presents, always watching, not my face but my hands. You looked forward to my visits because of the happy feelings you had when I told you you should be a princess in my Court. It was yourself you thought of all the time of my visit, and when you blamed the clock for going too fast, it was because it was taking away a happy time *for you,* a time of *feeling* happy. I want to teach you now that feelings do not matter.

"When my visits make you feel happy, you may be glad, of course. But when you are tired, or out of sorts in any way and can find nothing to say to me, and if I say little to you, do not think it is always because I am displeased. If you know you have disappointed me or been shabby with me when I asked for some little sacrifice, be sorry and make it up to me by some loving words. Never mind if you don't *feel* loving; feelings do not count. Tell me you cannot give me any because you haven't any, talk to me as well as you can, and bear patiently the pain that you feel. Tell me your poor little heart is sad and lonely. I know you so well. I know what you would like to say to me. If you cannot say it, cannot say or do anything, well, never mind; I shall know all the same. You are staying quietly beside me. You are giving me a safe shelter in your hut, and though you think that because I am silent, I am doing nothing here, I am more busy than you can guess. You will know that some day when you see me, not in my disguise but as they see me in the Golden City."

"Dear King, if only I could see you so now I think I should feel more love for you and could give you a better welcome."

"The feelings you shall have some day, Dilecta, and your welcome is never more pleasing to me than when you are content to love me for myself and not just for the happy feelings I give sometimes. Remember this, else you might stay away from me because my visits did not make you *feel happy.* Know they make me happy and let that be enough for you now."

So Dilecta comforted herself with the thought that the King did not mind feelings, and was quite contented if she did her best. "She hath done what she could," he had said of one of his friends, when he paid her a visit long ago. He said the same many a time of his little Dilecta, for the invitations were always the same whether there were feelings or not. She never let him miss a visit, because she knew he wanted to come, and if only she could please him she was content. But though she was willing to wait, she longed more and more for the time when she could see the King as the Happy Ones see him and love him as she desired.

The King told her that he was more busy in the quiet silent visits than she suspected. He was indeed. It was his frequent visits—they came at last to be daily—that made her training go on fast and so well, that her Prince Guardian scarcely recognized her as the little selfish thing she was once.

19

The King in His Beauty

THE time was at hand for that training to come to an end.

Whenever the King came now, she had always the same question for him:

"Dear King, will it be today?"

And his answer was the same always:

"Watch! Be ready! For you know not the day nor the hour. I do not say, 'Be getting ready', but—'*Be ready*'!"

So she tried to have all in order. The little hut was always well swept, the window clean and bright, the jar of wild flowers ready for him when he came. When at daybreak she rose to her day's work, she would cheer herself with the thought: "Before evening maybe I shall be with him." And at night as she lay down to rest, she would think: "Perhaps before morning he will come." All her work, all her little kindnesses, were done to please him. All her pains and troubles were borne cheerfully for his sake, and to pay her debts here, so that she might be ready to go to him straight, or at least without any long stay in the Land of Weary Waiting.

Such was her haste to be with him, to see him in all his beauty as he was seen in the Golden City, that often when evening came and her work was done, she would take her telescope and try to see dimly the gleam of its gold and precious stones and its glistening gates of pearl! And she would sing:

"Ah, my sweet Home, Jerusalem,
  Would God I were in thee:
Would God my woes were at an end,
  Thy joys that I might see!"

She knew that she was not yet beyond the reach of her enemies. Malignus was still busy prowling about. The Triflers had not given up hopes of making her one of themselves . . . yet.

"And what about Self?" you will ask. "Had Dilecta forgotten her?" Hardly. It is not easy for that personage to be forgotten long. Poor Self! I am not surprised at your being interested in her. Most people are. If we have not heard so much about her of late, it has simply been because there was less to tell. All things considered, she had turned out better than might have been expected. Little by little she learned to know her place, which is saying a good deal for one so inclined to be forward and to give herself airs. True, she was always at hand, but less troublesome, less given to arguing, more easily silenced and made to do as she was told. She came at length to understand the meaning of that short word "No," and to put up with what it meant, if not with a good grace always, at least with patience. In short, she was better behaved in every respect. Mind you, she had to be watched up to the very end, and every now and then she was caught at her old pranks. But I think we may say that she turned out a credit to her trainer, and Dilecta looked

forward to finding her quite a pleasant companion in the Palace of the King.

One day the King came to the hut for the last time. It was to fetch the little maid. She had done what he required of her. She had made up her mind to reach the Golden City and to be with the King always—at any cost. And so she had let herself be trained by him and by those who held his place, and she had herself helped bravely in the training, as we have seen. And now the work was finished. She was fit to be a Princess in his Court—and he had come for her.

And they went out of the hut together, and down, down into the Dark Valley that lay between the Land of Exile and the Beautiful Land beyond. Terrible things were in that darkness, but the King kept his arm round her and held her fast that no harm might come to her. They crossed the Valley and passed into the Beautiful Land. And as they neared the Golden City there floated over the gates of pearl, a song from within:

> *"Lift up your gates, ye Princes,*
> *and the King of Glory shall enter in!"*

And the gates of pearl lifted, and a great radiance streamed out. And in the midst stood One whom the little maid knew. His disguise had fallen from Him, and . . . there He was, as He had promised she should see Him, as she had so longed to see

Him, face to face! She saw the King in His beauty . . . and was satisfied.

And He brought her into the Golden City and made her welcome there, in return for His many welcomes to the little hut in the days gone by. And when she beheld the crowd of Princes and Princesses who waited on Him, clad in robes of dazzling whiteness, and the majesty and beauty of the King Himself, she cried out: "O King of Glory, how could You have so loved me as to come in your disguise to the little hut far away! Oh that I had known You better and loved You more!"

The End

THE Little Way Press publishes classic tales and creative, hands-on materials that guide young hearts along the *little way of love.*

Other titles from Little Way Press:
A Catholic How-to-Draw by Andrea Smith
Sewing with Saint Anne by Alice Cantrell
A Year with God: Celebrating the Liturgical Year
Rare Catholic Stories and Poems
The Little Apostle on Crutches by Henriette Delamare
And more

Contact our distributor to learn more about
Little Way books:
Catholic Heritage Curricula
P.O. Box 125
Twain Harte, California 95383

To request a free catalog, call toll-free: 1-800-490-7713
Or visit online: www.chcweb.com